STEGOSAURUS

COMPSOGNATHUS

TRICERATOPS

JURAVENATOR

To _____

From _____

Date _____

BRONTOSAURUS

IGUANODON

PLESIOSAURUS

VELOCIRAPTOR

STEGOSAURUS

DILOPHOSAURUS

TRICERATOPS

COMPSOGNATHUS

JURAVENATOR

BRONTOSAURUS

IGUANODON

PLESIOSAURUS

VELOCIRAPTOR

A VERY DINOSAUR BIRTHDAY

ADAM WALLACE

Art by
CHRISTOPHER NIELSEN

Tommy NELSON

An Imprint of Thomas Nelson
thomasnelson.com

Published in Nashville, Tennessee, by Tommy Nelson. Tommy Nelson is an imprint of Thomas Nelson. Thomas Nelson is a registered trademark of HarperCollins Christian Publishing, Inc.

Tommy Nelson titles may be purchased in bulk for educational, business, fundraising, or sales promotional use. For information, please e-mail SpecialMarkets@ThomasNelson.com.

ISBN 978-1-4002-4204-7 (eBook)
ISBN 978-1-4002-4206-1 (audiobook)

Library of Congress Cataloging-in-Publication Data

Names: Wallace, Adam, author. | Nielsen, Christopher, 1973- illustrator.
Title: A very dinosaur birthday / Adam Wallace ; art by Christopher Nielsen.
Description: Nashville, Tennessee : Tommy Nelson, [2023] | Audience: Ages 4-10. | Summary: Illustrations and rhyming text show what to expect when dinosaurs show up at your birthday party, from their bringing moldy presents to their eating all the food.
Identifiers: LCCN 2022055886 (print) | LCCN 2022055887 (ebook) | ISBN 9781400242054 (hardcover) | ISBN 9781400242047 (epub)
Subjects: CYAC: Stories in rhyme. | Dinosaurs--Fiction. | Birthday parties--Fiction. | LCGFT: Stories in rhyme. | Picture books.
Classification: LCC PZ8.3.W15844 Ve 2023 (print) | LCC PZ8.3.W15844 (ebook) | DDC [E]--dc23
LC record available at https://lccn.loc.gov/2022055886
LC ebook record available at https://lccn.loc.gov/2022055887

Written by Adam Wallace

Illustrated by Christopher Nielsen

Printed in India

23 24 25 26 27 REP 10 9 8 7 6 5 4 3 2 1

Mfr: REP / Sonipat, India / May 2023 / PO #12167144

For Mum. Thanks for listening to the drafts of this story. You couldn't move because your back was broken, but thanks anyway!
—Adam

For Oma and her perfect Eden.
—CN

CHRISILLOTOPS   WALLOSAURUS REX

Dinosaurs are **BIG** and strong.
They're clumsy and they're
FARTY.

HAPPY

So do you *really* want them coming to your birthday party?

If they bring you presents, they will probably be old.

And STINKY. And BROKEN.

And covered in

MOLD.

Dinosaurs love hide-and-seek,
but finding them's no fun.

The Brontosaurus hides its head
but not its  bum!

When it's time for pass the parcel,
T. rex will come last.
His TINY arms can't grab the parcel
as the parcel's passed!

Pinning tails on donkeys
is fun for one and all.

But a DIZZY Ankylosaurus
will crash right through your wall.

If your birthday's at a pool,
that would be a **WIN**.
Except that there's no water
once a dinosaur **JUMPS** in!

Dinos are polite.

They don't want to be rude.

But in one **MIGHTY MOUTHFUL**, they have eaten all the food!

Blowing out the candles
can be done with style and grace.

But if a dino helps, the cake will

DECORATE

your face!

You thought a DINO BIRTHDAY PARTY would be just the best. But you're so stressed, you trudge up to your bedroom for a rest.

Triceratops feels bad and wants
to give your mood a lift.

UH
OH! It barged into your room . . .
and now it's broken *every* gift!

They want to make you happy.
They know just what to do.
And so they play a game of catch.

You do some

FINGER PAINTING.

They make a birthday card.
But since they don't have fingers,
finger painting's rather hard.

This really is becoming the coolest party ever seen.
Especially when a dino tummy is a TRAMPOLINE!

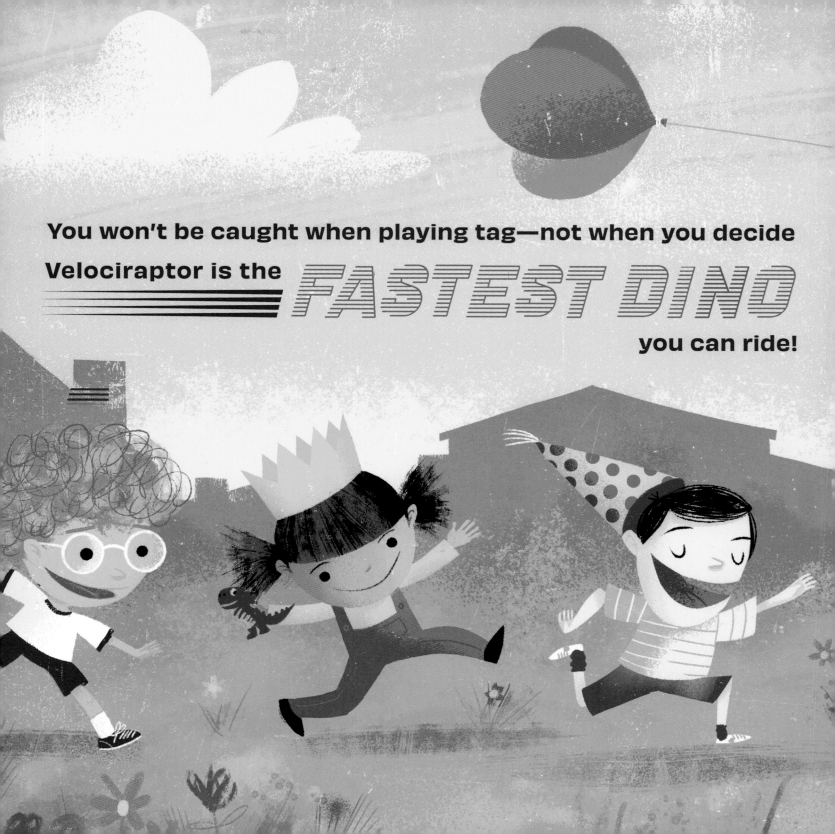

You won't be caught when playing tag—not when you decide Velociraptor is the **FASTEST DINO** you can ride!

Your party was amazing!

And if you **ASK AND ASK** all year,

perhaps the

DINOS

can come back

for extra Christmas cheer!

ALLOSAURUS

ABELISAURUS

PTERODACTYL

TROODON

DIMETRODON

ANKYLOSAURUS

TYRANNOSAURUS
REX

BRACHIOSAURUS

ARCHAEOPTERYX

Celebrate Your Own

VERY DINOSAUR BIRTHDAY PARTY

INVITATIONS

Invite your friends with homemade cards and a fun dinosaur phrase.

★★★

Stomp, Chomp, and Roar! Party like a Dinosaur!

Breaking News! Dinosaurs have been spotted ... Join the discovery at [Your Name's] birthday party

★★★

You're Invited to [Your Name's] Dino-Mite Birthday Party

Prehistoric Party Time!

 ## DECORATIONS

Turn your party room into a Jurassic jungle with green balloons and streamers.

Cut out giant footprints from brown poster board to create a trail of dinosaur tracks.

Scatter whole coconuts and post a sign:

WATCH YOUR STEP— DINO DROPPINGS!